ALL DIFFERENT AND BEAUTIFUL

A Children's Book about Diversity, Kindness, and Friendships

Written by

Belle Belrose

Illustrated by

Winna CL

ISBN 978-3-949152-00-9 (paperback)
ISBN 978-3-949152-01-6 (hardcover)

Be different, be kind, and be brave.

Be YOU!

Dedicated to my parents, Jana and Peter.

Orion was new to America. He was a confident, bright little boy.
Orion was friendly and knew how to share—even a shiny new toy.

Whenever Orion saw somebody sad, he tried to do all that he could.
He learned from his parents that helping out and lending a hand was good.

Although he was going to a brand-new school, Orion did not feel afraid.
He knew he was capable, friendly, and kind, and he knew just how friendships are made.

He showed up to school with a spring in his step and a grin on his bright, happy face.
Orion was happy 'cause every day he made the world a more beautiful place.

The first friend he met when he got to the school was Emma—who looked sad that day. She was very lonely, 'cause just like Orion, she moved here from far, far away.

"Hello!" said Orion to Emma. But Emma was nervous about answering him back. "I don't like to talk because English is hard," Emma said. Her voice started to crack.

Orion, however, knew just what to say. "Emma, I also learned to speak better. And learning new languages is kind of fun—if you want, we can practice together!"

Emma smiled and said, "That's so nice of you. Let's practice when this class ends!" And that's how Orion connected with Emma, and now they are very good friends.

Just three days later, Orion met someone else who looked so terribly shy.
His name was Joaquin, and his clothing was old. Orion was wondering why.

"Hello!" said Orion. But Joaquin looked through his thick glasses down at the floor.
Orion knew something was bothering him, so he started to talk to him more.

"My name is Orion," he said. "And I really like your green corduroy pants!"
Joaquin looked up, and he mumbled, "But they are so old they might rip if I dance!"

"Then why do you wear them if you do not like them?" Orion asked, looking confused.
"Because," said Joaquin, "both my parents are poor, so our clothing is old, and it's used."

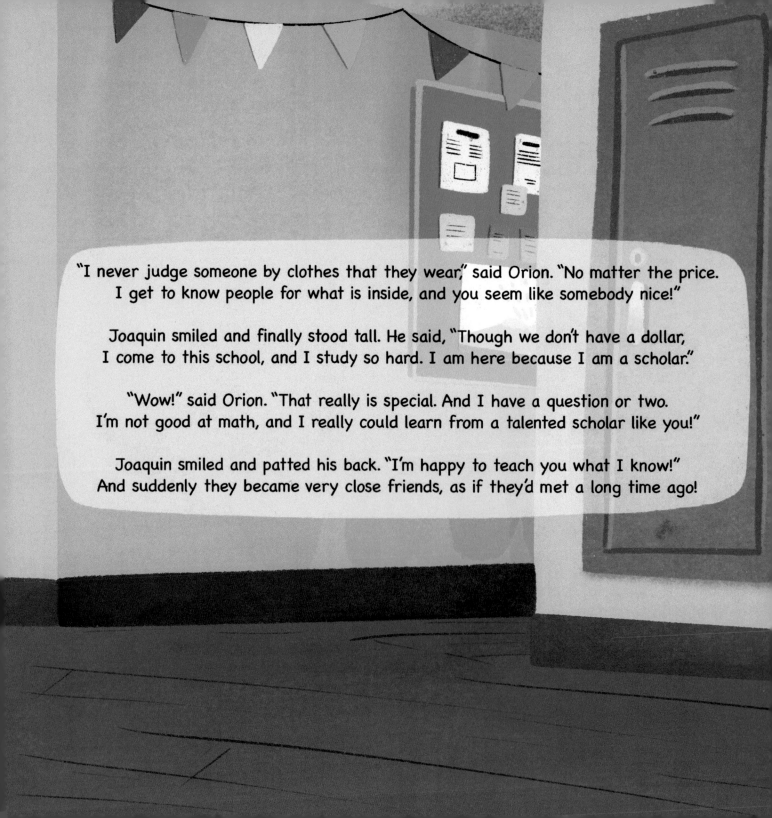

"I never judge someone by clothes that they wear," said Orion. "No matter the price.
I get to know people for what is inside, and you seem like somebody nice!"

Joaquin smiled and finally stood tall. He said, "Though we don't have a dollar,
I come to this school, and I study so hard. I am here because I am a scholar."

"Wow!" said Orion. "That really is special. And I have a question or two.
I'm not good at math, and I really could learn from a talented scholar like you!"

Joaquin smiled and patted his back. "I'm happy to teach you what I know!"
And suddenly they became very close friends, as if they'd met a long time ago!

One day when Orion was walking through school, he bumped into a girl near the stairs. He'd seen her in class, but they'd never yet spoke, and she sat in a pink wheelchair.

"Excuse me," he said. "Hey, I don't think I met you before. I'm new to this school." He looked at her wheelchair. "How did you get one in pink? That is so very cool!"

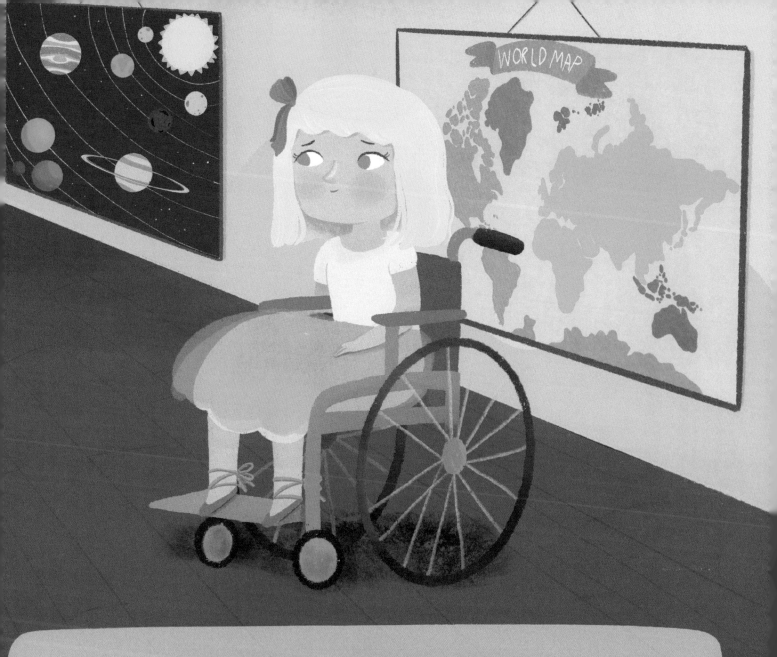

The girl smiled shyly. "My name is Sofia," she said. "Yes, I've seen you before. I wanted to talk to you, but then I got scared and wheeled my way out the door."

"Why did you leave?"asked Orion. "I always like making new friends, every day!"
"Me too," said Sofia, "but sometimes my wheelchair scares other children away."

"It doesn't scare me!" said Orion. "Besides, I bet you can zoom by really fast!"
Then he and Sofia both giggled, and they had a friendship that always would last.

Every day, Axel made jokes in the classroom. He certainly was the class clown! And every day, all of the teachers reminded him, "Please, Axel—please, settle down!"

All the kids laughed when he went through his antics. They giggled at all of his jokes. Orion, however, thought maybe his silliness was just a cover-up hoax.

One day in the lunchroom, he saw Axel sitting alone, so he went to say hi.
"My name is Orion," he said. "Why do you look so sad, like you might cry?"

Axel said, "Nobody knows the reason why I'm always playing those games.
It's 'cause I don't like myself all that much, and I just feel so sad and ashamed!"

"Why's that?" asked Orion. "I think you're a very nice person, Axel. You have a good heart."
But Axel just sadly said, "Other boys like to play sports, and I don't. I like art."

"So what?" asked Orion. "Each person is different and likes different things—it's okay!
And, Axel, I also like art! Will you come to my house and paint with me one day?"

Axel's eyes brightened. "I really would like that! But wait, aren't you friends now with Buzz? He doesn't like art, and I also think that you don't like to play the same sports as he does."

"Well, yes," said Orion. "But we can be friends even if we don't like the same stuff. We're friends because Buzz and I both like each other, and Axel, that's always enough!"

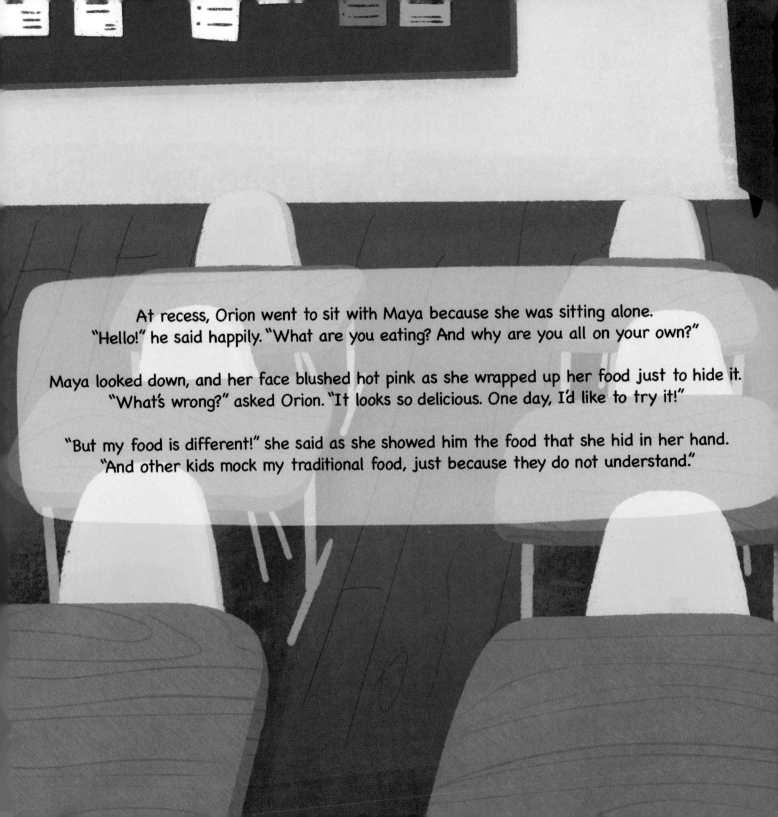

At recess, Orion went to sit with Maya because she was sitting alone.
"Hello!" he said happily. "What are you eating? And why are you all on your own?"

Maya looked down, and her face blushed hot pink as she wrapped up her food just to hide it.
"What's wrong?" asked Orion. "It looks so delicious. One day, I'd like to try it!"

"But my food is different!" she said as she showed him the food that she hid in her hand.
"And other kids mock my traditional food, just because they do not understand."

fajita

falafel

donuts

hamburger

summer rolls

dumplings

corn on the cob

pizza

nachos

fried tempeh

soup

sushi

pretzel

"Our lives are more flavorful and more exciting when we share our culture with others. I wish that we all could try lots of traditional foods and eat with one another."

Maya said, "Maybe you're right. Would you like to try sharing my snack? Take a bite!" Orion and Maya were friends now, and both of their smiles shone, sparkling and bright.

Nova was also a girl in the class, but she struggled to play and fit in.
Orion asked why, and she said, "I am different because of my hair and my skin."

"Your skin and your hair might be different," he answered. "They might even set you apart.
But what makes you special, for real, is all of the goodness you have in your heart!"

Nova looked up at Orion and asked, "Do you really believe that is true?"
Orion said, "Yes, Nova. It's the truth. I believe it—I certainly do!"

"Orion," she smiled. "You are unique, and you have a very big, beautiful heart.
I hope we'll be friends," Nova said. And they were—they were of to a wonderful start!

Orion played with all the children around him—each kid in his class was his friend!
He found something special inside each and every one, long before the school year's end.

And then, on the very last school day, the class was enjoying the summery air.
Orion said, "Our teacher's birthday is coming—I think that we all should be there!"

"Let's throw a party!" the friends all decided. "Let's make sure her birthday is great!"
Orion said, "I'll make a present for her. This will be so much fun—I can't wait!"

Emma said, "I'll decorate for the party!" Sofia said, "I'll bake a cake!"
Joaquin said, "I'll bring lots of music to play!" Maya said, "I'll bring food that I make!"

Axel said, "I'll entertain everybody—I'll make a big, huge celebration!"
And Nova said, "I will make sure we're all there—I will send everyone invitations!"

And when the last bell rang, the kids looked around at each other, and all of them knew:
The party—and life!—is more special 'cause each different person brings something beautiful and new.

We hope that you and your kid(s) enjoyed the book. It would mean a lot to the author and us if you **please leave a review**—even if it's just a sentence or two. It makes all the difference and is very much appreciated.

If you want to be the first to know about our new releases and giveaways, follow us on Facebook or Instagram @8BCpublishing.

New book in the Orion Series:

Verses of Kindness, Self-Compassion, and Mindful Affirmations for Kids

Search for the ISBN: 978-3949152245

Made in the USA
Middletown, DE
03 October 2023

40111344R00020